Camilla
the Christmas Present
Fairy

Special thanks to
Rachel Elliot

ORCHARD BOOKS

First published in Great Britain in 2019 by The Watts Publishing Group

1 3 5 7 9 10 8 6 4 2

© 2019 Rainbow Magic Limited.
© 2019 HIT Entertainment Limited.
Illustrations © Orchard Books 2019

A CIP catalogue record for this book is available from the British Library.

ISBN 978 1 40835 246 5

Printed and bound in Great Britain by Clays Ltd, Elcograf S.p.A.

MIX
Paper from
responsible sources
FSC® C104740

The paper and board used in this book are made from wood from responsible sources

Orchard Books
An imprint of Hachette Children's Group
Part of The Watts Publishing Group Limited
Carmelite House, 50 Victoria Embankment, London EC4Y 0DZ

An Hachette UK Company
www.hachette.co.uk
www.hachettechildrens.co.uk

Camilla
the Christmas Present Fairy

By Daisy Meadows

ORCHARD

www.rainbowmagicbooks.co.uk

The Fairyland Palace

Tippington High Street

Doughnuts

Mount Everest
Toy Workshop

Jack Frost's
Ice Castle

Tippington Town

Contents

Story One:

The Glowing List

Chapter One: An Unexpected Gift   11
Chapter Two: Muddled Minds   21
Chapter Three: Snow Clue   29
Chapter Four: Hair Care   39
Chapter Five: The Grand Battle   49

Story Two:
The Glittering Bow

Chapter Six: Oh, Buttons!   61
Chapter Seven: The Snow Cloud Sleigh   71
Chapter Eight: One Hundred Elves   81
Chapter Nine: Pink Plaits   89
Chapter Ten: A Mysterious Bauble   97

Story Three:
The Golden Present

Chapter Eleven: Grumpy Elves   111
Chapter Twelve: Reindeer Rescue   119
Chapter Thirteen: Frozen Fairy   129
Chapter Fourteen: Tower of Troublemakers   137
Chapter Fifteen: Friends For Ever   145

Jack Frost's Spell

I am very proud to be
Grasping, grabby, selfish me.
I'll take Camilla's things and shout:
"That's what Christmas is about!"

Toys and trinkets, gifts galore,
Shower me with more and more.
Gimme! Gimme! I want stuff.
I'll never say I have enough!

Story One
The Glowing List

Chapter One
An Unexpected Gift

"Hurry up, train," said Kirsty Tate under her breath. "I am longing to see Rachel!"

Kirsty was going to spend the week before Christmas with her best friend Rachel Walker in Tippington. They had shared many adventures, and Kirsty knew that she was going to have a wonderful week.

Kirsty peeped into her present bag with Christmassy excitement. It was bulging with gifts. Her favourite one was the friendship bracelet that she had made for Rachel. Then she noticed that the label had fallen off.

"Bother," she murmured.

She felt around in the bottom of the bag and pulled out a label. It said: *To Mrs Walker, love from Kirsty.*

"Oh no," said Kirsty. "All the labels have come off. I hope I can remember whose is whose."

Then she noticed a small gift wrapped in crackly gold paper.

"I don't remember wrapping that," she said.

Suddenly the gold paper started to sparkle. Twinkling silver lights flickered across it like distant stars. Could it be . . .

"Magic?" Kirsty whispered.

Ever since the day she and Rachel had

met on Rainspell Island, fairy magic
had been a part of their friendship. But
usually their fairy friends appeared when
they were together. Kirsty reached out
and touched the crackly paper.

At once, a honey-coloured glow spread
across the present. The gold paper curled
outwards, and Kirsty saw a tiny fairy
waving up at her.

"Hello, Kirsty," she whispered. "I'm Camilla the Christmas Present Fairy."

Camilla was wearing a dark blue dress embellished with silver stars, and had a matching silver star tiara in her hair. Her eyes sparkled even more brightly than the gold paper, and she had a glittering earpiece tucked behind her ear.

Kirsty glanced around. The carriage was empty apart from one lady who was fast asleep.

"Hello, Camilla," Kirsty said. "I'm sorry Rachel isn't here too. I'm on my way to stay with her."

"I know," said Camilla. "That's why I'm here! You see, Ja k Frost has stolen my magical objects. Holly the Christmas Fairy said I should ask you and Rachel for help. Jack Frost sent his goblins to

15

Tippington to stop me. So I decided to join you before you reached Tippington."

"I'm so glad you did," said Kirsty, smiling. "Tell me what happened."

"I'll show you," said Camilla.

She pointed her wand at the train window. Kirsty's reflection melted into a sparkling mist, and then she saw Jack Frost tiptoeing towards a huge Christmas tree. It was brimming with baubles, candy canes, sugared nuts and silver bells. There were garlands of tiny mirrors, and little candles that made the tinsel glimmer.

"That's the Christmas tree in the palace, where I keep my magical objects," said Camilla.

Kirsty watched the cloaked figure creep up to the Christmas tree and pick three decorations from its branches. He tucked

them into his cloak and then rubbed his bony hands together. The picture faded.

"Were those decorations your magical objects?" Kirsty asked.

"Yes," said Camilla. "They help me to make Christmas presents perfect. The glowing list tells me what each person would like best. The glittering bow makes presents look lovely, and the golden present inspires people to be generous. Without them, presents all over the world will be a disaster."

"Rachel and I will find a way to get your magical objects back," Kirsty promised the little fairy.

Just then, she felt the train slowing

down. Camilla hid under Kirsty's hair as the train slid into Tippington's brightly painted station. On the platform, Rachel was jumping up and down and waving like mad.

"Hurray!" Kirsty heard her shouting. "You're here at last!"

Chapter Two
Muddled Minds

The train doors opened, and Kirsty stepped out and flung her arms around her best friend.

"We're going to have so much fun," said Rachel.

"Even more than you think," Kirsty whispered in her ear. "Camilla the

Christmas Present Fairy is hiding under my hair."

"Wow, really?" said Rachel. "It sounds like an adventure is just around the corner."

The best friends shared an excited smile.

"Hello, Kirsty," said Mrs Walker, hugging her. "Welcome to Tippington."

"There's a Christmas fair in the high street," Rachel told Kirsty as they walked to the car. "We thought you might like to go. Mum and Dad still have a few presents to buy, and we can talk about you know what."

After putting Kirsty's bags in the car, they all walked down the high street. Rachel was longing to say hello to Camilla, but she didn't mind waiting a little while so she could enjoy the

Christmas fair. The pavements were deep with powdery snow, and the aroma of roasted chestnuts, freshly cooked doughnuts and cinnamon filled the air. A choir was singing carols on a little stage. Stalls, rides and games jostled for space.

"Do you have the list?" Mrs Walker asked her husband. "I can't remember who we still need to buy presents for."

Mr Walker reached into his pocket. A puzzled look came over his face. He checked his other pockets.

"It's gone," he said. "I'm sorry. I'm sure I had it when we left home."

"Never mind," said Mrs Walker. "We'll just have to get the rest of the presents tomorrow instead."

As they turned back towards the car, Kirsty put her arm through Rachel's.

"There's a reason that list has gone missing," she whispered. "When we get to your house I'll tell you all about it."

As soon as the girls were in Rachel's bedroom, Camilla fluttered out of her hiding place. Together, she and Kirsty

explained what had happened.

"I said we'd help, of course," said Kirsty.

"Definitely," Rachel agreed. "We won't let Jack Frost spoil Christmas. I wonder what he wants to do with your magical objects."

"No idea at all," said Camilla, sinking down on to Rachel's pillow.

"What is that sparkly thing in your

ear?" Rachel asked.

Padma smiled brightly.

"It's my cochlear implant," she said. "It helps me to hear and talk to people. It was a present from Father Christmas. Oh dear, what am I going to tell him?"

Kirsty stared at Camilla in excitement.

"You work with Father Christmas?" she whispered.

Camilla nodded miserably.

"When he has checked who has been naughty and nice, my glowing list helps him decide which present to give each child," she explained. "I'm supposed to visit him tonight. He'll be so disappointed."

At that moment, they heard Mrs Walker's voice.

"Rachel, could you come down?" she

called. "I need help."

Camilla flew into Kirsty's pocket and the girls hurried downstairs. Mrs Walker was beside the Christmas tree, surrounded by unwrapped presents.

"I'm in such a muddle," she said, rubbing her forehead. "I can't remember who each of these presents is for. Did

I buy the wooden spoon for Aunt Ena or Uncle George? Was the apron for cousin Sara or cousin James?"

Rachel frowned at the presents.

"I feel as if my head is full of cotton wool," she said. "I don't remember who they're for either."

"I'll go and make a cup of tea," said Mrs Walker, standing up. "Perhaps that will clear my thoughts."

Rachel and Kirsty went to gaze out of the window. The snow was falling again.

"This is all happening because my list is missing," said Camilla with a sigh.

"Wait a minute," Kirsty whispered, pointing to some tracks that criss-crossed the garden. "Are those goblin footprints?"

They were! In a flash, the girls were

Chapter Three
Snow Clue

pulling on their wellies, coats and scarves.

"We're just going to enjoy the snow before it gets dark," Rachel called to her mother.

"OK," said Mrs Walker. "Be home in time for tea."

Outside, the snow was falling more

heavily than ever. The girls scrunched their way over to the footprints.

"There are two sets," said Rachel. "That means we're looking for two goblins. I wonder what they're doing in Tippington."

"Maybe they know I'm here to get

your help," whispered
Camilla. "Perhaps they
wanted to stop us from
meeting."

"The footprints will
soon be covered with
snow," said Kirsty. "We
have to hurry."

The footprints led them
towards the skate park. It
was empty apart from the
girls, so Camilla dared to
fly out of Kirsty's pocket.

"I just need to stretch
my wings," she said.

She fluttered upwards as
snowflakes twirled down
around her. She stopped
when she was level with

the top of a fir tree.

"Oh my goodness," she exclaimed. "I can see the goblins!"

She swooped down to the girls and pointed towards the skate park.

Rachel and Kirsty ran into the skate park. Two goblins were standing beside a ramp, arguing. They were wearing Christmas jumpers and Santa hats, and there was a rucksack in the snow between them.

Camilla tucked herself into Rachel's scarf. The girls crept up behind the ramp.

"He said he wanted an exciting present," they heard the shorter goblin say. "Socks aren't exciting."

"They are if your feet are cold," the taller goblin snapped. "My toes get very chilly in all the snow."

"We're not buying presents for you," squawked the shorter goblin. "You heard what he said – he wants some good presents for Christmas. He hasn't forgiven us for that fairy-shaped bath mat we gave him last year."

"Use the stupid list then," grumbled the other goblin.

The shorter goblin pulled a scroll from

under his hat. It glimmered as he unrolled it.

"That's my glowing list," Camilla cried. Rachel and Kirsty tiptoed closer, and saw golden writing appear on the scroll.

"What's that?" Rachel whispered.

"The list shows the presents each person most wants," Camilla explained. "The goblins are thinking about Jack Frost, so they will see a list of Jack Frost's perfect gifts."

The weather was getting worse. Kirsty blinked snowflakes out of her eyes.

"This means that Jack Frost will get exactly what he wants for Christmas," she said.

"Yes," said Camilla, flying out of

Rachel's scarf again. "But no one else
will. Presents will get mixed up and
people will get gifts that were meant for
someone else."

"What's first on the list?" asked the
taller goblin.

"Extra spiky hair gel," said the short
goblin. "Let's go!"

He put the glowing list into the rucksack, picked it up and stomped off.

"I'm tired," whined the bigger goblin, trailing after him. "I want to go home. I don't like shopping."

"Who said anything about shopping?" said the other goblin, grinning.

Rachel and Kirsty exchanged a worried glance.

"We have to follow them and get the glowing list back," said Rachel. "But how?"

Chapter Four
Hair Care

The goblins left the snowy skate park and headed towards Tippington town centre. Rachel and Kirsty followed the goblins along the high street and through the busy Christmas Fair.

"Where are they going?" Kirsty wondered.

The goblins stopped at a food stall and pulled faces at the man making the doughnuts.

"Clear off," said the man, looking grumpy.

Squawking and sniggering, the goblins darted across the road into the hairdressing salon, Tippington Tresses.

"Of course," said Rachel. "They're going to get extra-spiky hair gel for Jack Frost."

The two friends peered through the steamed-up window. At first they couldn't see the goblins. Then Kirsty gasped.

"I think they've been trying out the hair gel," she said.

Inside, the goblins were standing in front of a mirror. They were cackling with laughter at their reflections. Gel had

made their straggly hair stick up on end.

"We need to get them away from here before they cause trouble," said Rachel.

The girls pushed open the door and stepped inside. The smell of shampoo was sweet and fruity. Customers were chatting happily as hairdressers washed, trimmed and layered their hair. There was a pyramid of chocolates on the desk.

The label said 'Free to customers. Merry
Christmas!'

"I can't see the goblins," said Kirsty.

Suddenly there was a squeal from one
of the hairdressers.

"My lady's hair has gone green!" she
exclaimed.

"Who has cut the hair on all the wigs?"
shouted the owner.

Rachel and Kirsty could hear giggling
and running feet, but they still couldn't
see the goblins.

"Is it getting windy in here? Rachel
asked.

"Yes, and warmer too," Kirsty agreed.

"Too warm," said Camilla. "The goblins
have turned on all the hairdryers."

Hot air was blasting all around them.
Neat hairstyles were messed up, and

the cut hair on the floor was blown
everywhere.

"Find them, quick!" Kirsty shouted over
the noise.

"The chocolates are melting,"
exclaimed the owner. "Turn those

hairdryers off!"

Just as he said that, the goblins
scrambled out from under a chair. The
shorter goblin had a tube of hair gel in
his hand.

"They're stealing it!" cried Rachel.

"Oh no you don't," said the owner.

He leaned forward and took the tube
back. Howling with fury, the goblins
yanked the door open and ran back into
the street. Rachel and Kirsty were after
them in a flash. The goblins zigzagged
through the crowd and out of the high
street. In a moment they were running
across a snowy field.

"They're quicker than us," said Rachel,
panting.

"Let's slow them down," Kirsty cried.

She grabbed a handful of snow and

threw it at the taller goblin. It landed on his head and flattened his spiky hair.

"Hey, my hairdo!" he yelled.

He bent down and made a large snowball, then sent it zooming towards Kirsty. She jumped aside, and Rachel whispered to Camilla.

"We'll keep them busy with a snowball fight," she said. "You fly into the rucksack and get the glowing list back."

It was a risky plan, but it was their best chance. Snowballs whizzed through the

air, smashing hard against trees, bushes – and sometimes each other. Meanwhile, Camilla fluttered around behind the goblins. Rachel noticed the little fairy's cochlear implant sparkling as she slipped inside the rucksack. Unluckily, so did the taller goblin!

Chapter Five
The Grand Battle

The goblin pounced on the rucksack and did up the straps.

"Ha ha, you're trapped!" he shouted.

Rachel and Kirsty ran towards the goblins. Instead of asking them to let Camilla go, Kirsty had another idea.

"Wait!" she called as they turned to

run. "That snowball fight was fun. Would you like to learn how to make snow angels?"

"Ooh, yes," said the goblins, forgetting all about leaving.

"It's really easy," said Kirsty, winking at Rachel. "You just have to lie down in the snow like this."

She lay down on her back.

"Then you move your arms up and down and your legs from side to side," she went on.

She jumped up and showed the goblin a perfect snow angel. Giggling, the goblins lay down in the snow.

"Ow!" squawked the smaller goblin. "This silly rucksack is digging into my back."

"Take it off for a minute," said the

other goblin.

The rucksack was flung aside.

"Hee hee, it's working," the shorter goblin cackled.

Kirsty glanced at Rachel, who understood at once. She darted over to the rucksack and opened it.

"I've got it!" cried Camilla.

She zoomed out of the rucksack, holding the glowing list high above her head. It had shrunk back to fairy size. The goblins were still making snow angels with Kirsty, and hadn't noticed Camilla escaping.

The little fairy fluttered beside Rachel's ear.

"Thank you from the bottom of my heart," she whispered. "Because of you two girls, my visit to Father Christmas will be a success. I can't wait to find out what he's going to give to each child. And look – even the goblins are having fun."

Rachel smiled. There were already ten snow angels on the field.

"Are you going to see Father Christmas right now?" she asked.

"Yes," said Camilla. "Is it all right if I come back afterwards? I'm sure I'll need your help to find the glittering bow and the golden present."

"Of course it's all right," said Rachel. "We couldn't bear to let anything spoil the fun of giving the perfect presents."

"Thank you," said Camilla. "You're wonderful friends."

"We'll see you soon," said Rachel. "Please give Father Christmas our love."

Camilla waved and disappeared in a flurry of flickering twinkles. Rachel ran to join Kirsty. The goblins had stopped making snow angels and were starting to

build a snow goblin. They were already quarrelling.

"Make the nose more pointy."

"No, the head should be bumpier, like mine."

"If it looks like you, it'll scare people."

"I think they've forgotten all about the glowing list," said Kirsty.

"Good," said Rachel as she scooped

up a big handful of snow. "That means
we've got just enough time."

"Time for what?" asked Kirsty.

"Time for fun," said Rachel, sending a huge snowball whizzing towards her best friend. "Snowball fun!"

Story Two
The Glittering Bow

Chapter Six
Oh, Buttons!

"That was the best game ever," giggled Kirsty, running up the garden path to Rachel's house. "But I've got snow everywhere, even inside my T-shirt."

It was Kirsty's second day staying with Rachel, and the girls had spent all morning building snow houses and snow castles in the Walkers' garden.

"Brrr, and I've got some in my boots," said Rachel, stamping her feet on the doormat. "My poor snowy toes!"

Blowing on their icy fingers, they opened the door and went inside. The house was warm and filled with the scent of freshly baked mince pies and gingerbread. Mr Walker came out of the kitchen, wiping his hands on a tea towel.

"You're just in time for lunch," he said. "We're going to have a floor picnic by the fire, and then wrap some presents."

"Brilliant idea," said Kirsty, shivering.

It was a feast! There were baked potatoes topped with cheese, sweetcorn and beans, cups of creamy tomato soup, toasted cheese sandwiches, warm butternut squash salad, dips with triangles

of pitta bread and chewy chocolate chip cookies to finish.

When no one could eat another bite, the girls helped to clear away. Then the presents were laid out and Mr Walker put a large flowery box on the table.

"This is our Christmas wrapping box,"

he told Kirsty. "It's where we keep all the things we need to make presents look pretty."

The girls peeped inside. There were sheets of brightly patterned paper, and bags of shiny foil bows in green, red, gold and silver. Glossy ribbons and squares of pastel-coloured organza lay beside neat piles of tags, tied together with silver thread.

"It really feels like Christmas when this box comes out," said Rachel, smiling.

She chose a sheet of green wrapping paper sprinkled with holly berries, and picked up a book from the present pile.

"Oh bother," she said as she folded the paper around the book. "I've made it all wonky."

"Never mind," said Mr Walker, putting

it straight for her. "That's fine. Now you can tape it."

But when Rachel put the tape on the paper, it stuck to itself and curled over in a messy lump. Kirsty tried to help, and the paper tore.

"I'm really sorry, Dad," said Rachel. "I've spoiled the lovely paper."

"It's OK," said Mr Walker. "Here, help me tie this ribbon."

The girls tried to help, but it seemed to spring out of their hands. Mr Walker tied the knot too loosely, and the ribbon drooped off the present he was wrapping.

"Oh dear," he said with a laugh. "We're not doing very well, are we?"

He picked up a bow and it fell apart in his hand.

"WOOF!"

Rachel's Old English Sheepdog, Buttons, scampered into the room.

"Buttons, no!" cried Rachel.

But it was too late. There were paw prints

all over the presents that the Walkers
had already wrapped, and one delicate
present was dented. Rachel took Buttons
by the collar and hurried him out of the
room.

"We're all excited about Christmas," she
whispered to him. "But that was a bit too
excited."

"WOOF!" said Buttons again, giving

her a big lick.

"I can't find the scissors," said Mr Walker. "And, oh dear, now the tape has run out. Where did I put that new roll?"

Rachel stood in the doorway and exchanged a worried glance with her best friend. Two of Camilla's magical objects were still missing. No wonder

they were having such trouble wrapping
the presents! Kirsty thought about the
friendship bracelet she had made for
Rachel.

"Please don't let anything spoil that,"
she murmured.

Rachel noticed that a gold bow had
fallen under the table. When she went
to pick it up, it started to glow. Was it
Camilla?

Chapter Seven
The Snow Cloud Sleigh

It was! The gold bow unravelled and the Christmas Present Fairy peeped out of the shiny foil.

"We have to go to the toy workshop," she whispered, fluttering into Rachel's pocket.

"Kirsty, please could you come

upstairs?" Rachel said, crawling out from under the table. "There's something I want to show you."

As soon as they were in Rachel's room, Camilla flew out.

"Hurray!" said Kirsty.

"Why are we going to a toy workshop?" Rachel asked.

"The elves have forgotten how to make presents look lovely, because Jack Frost stole my glittering bow," Camilla explained. "Without it, all wrapping will be wonky and messy, and no presents will be ready on Christmas Eve. Just imagine all those disappointed children on Christmas morning."

Rachel and Kirsty couldn't bear to think about it!

"The chief elf sent me a magical message this morning," Camilla went on. "Look."

She gave her wand a little flick, and a sheet of paper unrolled from it like a flag. A message was written in sparkling red letters:

73

The elves are in an awful flap.
We can't remember how to wrap!
Even worse, the youngest elf
saw goblins climbing on a shelf.
The workshop's full of fear and worry.
We need your help at once: please hurry!

"Let's go right now," Rachel exclaimed. "If the goblins are there, perhaps we can get the glittering bow back."

Just then, the curtain billowed and an icy blast of air swept into the room. Rachel hurried to shut the window. Then Camilla tucked herself under Kirsty's hair and the girls ran downstairs.

"Mum, is it OK if we go outside?"

Rachel called as she pulled on her wellies.

"Again?" said Mrs Walker in surprise. "You two really love the snow! Yes, you may go."

Wrapped up in scarves, gloves, coats and bobble hats, the girls hurried out into the garden. Kirsty pointed to the largest bush, which was covered in a thick layer of snow.

"Let's hide behind there," she suggested.
As soon as they were hidden, Camilla
fluttered out and raised her wand.

*"These girls and I must journey far,
To where the Christmas workshops are.
The chief elf needs our help today,
So take us swiftly on our way."*

Swirls of golden
fairy dust tumbled
from her wand.
They danced across
the snow, lifting
and shaping it. In a
twinkling, a delicate
white sleigh was
standing in front of
them.

"It's a snow cloud sleigh," said Camilla.

Eagerly, Rachel and Kirsty climbed in. They sank into the soft, white seats and cosy cloud blankets snuggled around them. Camilla slipped into the space between the girls. Just then, Rachel heard a squawk. She turned, but there was no one there.

"Did you hear something?" she asked Kirsty.

Kirsty shook her head and snuggled deeper into the cloud blanket.

The sleigh rose into the air and the girls leaned over the side, looking down at Rachel's house. There was a group of children building snowmen in a nearby garden.

"What if someone looks up?" asked Kirsty.

77

"Most human eyes can't see this magical sleigh," said Camilla. "You can see it because you have the fairy dust in the lockets Queen Titania gave you."

The sleigh rose higher and higher. The air got colder, but the girls were warm under the cloud blankets. Soon they were so high that the children in the garden looked like tiny specks on the snow.

"Hold on tight," said Camilla. "We'll be there in two shakes of a reindeer's tail!"

Chapter Eight
One Hundred Elves

WHOOSH! The sleigh zoomed across the sky. The girls squealed, their hair streaming out behind them.

"We're going faster than those cars," Kirsty said, gazing down at the snaking roads.

"Faster than I can fly," said Camilla.

They felt light and dizzy. It was a bit like riding a rollercoaster.

"Look up ahead," cried Kirsty.

"Are they mountains or clouds?" asked Rachel.

It was hard to tell! One moment they looked like puffy heaps of cotton wool. The next moment, the girls saw ice glinting on mountaintops. The sleigh wheeled around the peak and landed on a platform made of glittering ice. As they landed, Kirsty thought she heard a cackle of laughter.

"Did you hear that?" she asked Rachel and Camilla.

Camilla checked that her implant was working, but Rachel shook her head.

"What did you hear?" she asked.

Before Kirsty could reply, a huge door

slid open in the mountainside, and the platform was pulled into a large room with high, sloping walls.

"Welcome to the Mount Everest toy workshop," said Camilla.

It was a thrilling place. The walls were lined with shelves, all filled with brightly

coloured toys. There were teddies and dolls; kites; music boxes and hobby horses; diggers; planes; jars of coloured marbles, sledges; and many more wonderful things.

"There are magical toy workshops hidden all over the human world, getting ready for Christmas Eve," Camilla explained.

"Where are the elves?" Kirsty asked.

There were rows of red, green and yellow benches, with little painted stools tucked neatly underneath them. On the benches were small hammers and chisels, pots of paint and tubs filled with paintbrushes. But there wasn't an elf to be seen.

"They must be in the wrapping room," said Camilla. "When all the presents have been made, the elves wrap them up and put them in a big sack ready for Father

Christmas to collect."

"Let's go and find them," said Rachel.

As they hopped out of the sleigh, Camilla heard a giggle. She looked around, but she couldn't see anyone.

I must have imagined it, she thought. *Perhaps my implant is picking up tiny sounds because it's extra sensitive.*

She led the girls to a long pole. It disappeared through a large, round hole in the floor.

"It's like a pole in a fire station," said Kirsty.

"Right," said Camilla. "You know what to do!"

WHEEEE! First Rachel and then Kirsty slid down the pole. As they went, they heard raised voices.

"It sounds like an argument," said Rachel.

The voices got louder, and then the girls landed with a bump in an even bigger room. Instantly, the voices stopped. A hundred shocked elves turned to stare at them. Then a whisper rippled around the crowd.

"Humans," the girls heard them say. "Real, live human beings!"

Chapter Nine
Pink Plaits

Rachel tried to say hello, but it came out as a nervous squeak.

"It's OK," said Camilla, fluttering forwards. "Rachel and Kirsty are friends of Fairyland. I've asked them to help me. We came to see the chief elf."

There was a little scuffle at the back

of the room, and then one of the elves stepped out in front of the others. She had pink hair, and her plaits curved upwards in U shapes.

"Thank you for coming, Camilla," she said. "And welcome, Rachel and Kirsty. As you can see, we need your help."

She waved her hand around the room. It was similar to the one they had left, with benches in the middle and shelves lining the walls. But here, the benches were piled high with crumpled-up wrapping paper, tangled ribbons and bows, as well as broken scissors, scribbled tags and glue sticks without their lids. The shelves were filled with badly wrapped presents – the paper torn, the ribbons loose and not a single tag attached.

"We started to wrap the presents, but it was a disaster," said the chief elf. "The harder we tried, the worse the presents looked. That should be full by now."

She pointed to a huge sack in the corner. The girls guessed that it belonged to Father Christmas.

"Somehow, we have forgotten how to

wrap," the chief elf finished with a sigh.

"No you haven't," said Kirsty. "This is happening because Jack Frost stole Camilla's magical objects. As long as he has the glittering bow, no one will be able to make presents look special."

"Is that why the goblins broke in here?" the chief elf asked.

BANG! CRASH! CLATTER!

A terrible noise came from the room
above their heads. Rachel, Kirsty,
Camilla and a hundred elves looked up.

"The goblins are in the present room!"
the chief elf cried.

"I'll stop them," said Camilla.

She zoomed upwards and disappeared
through the hole in the ceiling. Kirsty
turned to Rachel, opening her locket.

"We can't let her go alone," she
declared.

She took a pinch
of fairy dust from
the locket and
sprinkled it over
her head. Rachel
did the same, and
magical sparkles
glimmered all around

them. The elves gasped as both girls
shrank to fairy size and grew filmy wings.

"I can't believe it," said the chief elf, rubbing her eyes.

"No time to explain!" said Rachel.

She and Kirsty zoomed after Camilla.

Chapter Ten
A Mysterious Bauble

Camilla was hovering in the present room in front of the shelves. Several toys were scattered on the floor. Two goblins stood opposite her, hopping from side to side, darting first one way and then the other to reach the toys. They squawked with laughter when Camilla tried to stop them.

"Too slow," sneered the first goblin, who had an ice-blue Christmas tree bauble dangling from one ear.

He knocked a doll on to the floor.

"Goblins!" exclaimed Rachel. "How did you get here?"

"We heard you say that there were goblins having fun here, and we wanted to join in," the goblin said. "So we hitched a lift on your silly sleigh."

"That explains the noises we heard," said Kirsty.

The second goblin jumped up and pulled a piggy bank off the shelf. It smashed, and the golden chocolate coins from inside rolled across the floor. The goblins screeched in delight.

"Please leave the toys alone," said Camilla, almost in tears.

Rachel and Kirsty darted to her side.

"Please stop," Kirsty cried. "The elves just want to wrap the presents up."

"They can't," said the first goblin, giggling.

He took the bauble from his ear and swung it from one finger as if he was gloating.

Rachel and Kirsty shared a confused glance. Why was he showing them a bauble?

"A bunch of fairies can't stop us," said the second goblin, sticking out his tongue.

"What about a very cross elf?" said a loud voice.

The chief elf was behind them, her pink plaits wobbling with anger and her hands on her hips. The first goblin stopped giggling.

"Don't shout at me," he snapped.

Rachel frowned at the ice-blue bauble in his hand. Why had he teased them with it?

"All we want to do is give children a merry Christmas," said the chief elf.

"And all we want to do is cause mischief," the goblin retorted. "That's our Christmas wish."

Rachel looked down at the gold chocolate coins that had fallen out of the pig. Then she looked at the goblin's bauble and gasped. Of course – she knew where the glittering bow was!

Swooping up to the lowest shelf, Rachel pushed every single marble jar on to the floor.

"Rachel!" cried Kirsty.

SMASH! The jars broke, and marbles scattered across the floor. The goblins were suddenly skating on a sea of marbles. They waved their arms around to get their balance, and the bauble flew into the air.

Rachel flew like the wind, and caught the bauble in her arms. Kirsty and Camilla stared at her in amazement as she carried it over to them.

"Touch it," she said to Camilla.

As soon as Camilla's hand rested on the bauble, it began to shimmer. Then it dissolved into a hundred tiny snowflakes that melted to nothing. Lying in Camilla's hand was a small bow, even more sparkly than her implant.

"My glittering bow!" she exclaimed.

The goblins scrambled away, and the chief elf whizzed down the pole to tell everyone the good news.

"I'm going to take the bow to
Fairyland, but I will come straight
back to help tidy up the toys and find
the golden present," Camilla promised
Rachel and Kirsty.

She vanished, leaving a few silvery
specks flickering in the air. A second later,
there was a cheer from the room below.

"I think that means the wrapping can start again," said Rachel. "Hurray!"

"Well done for guessing where the bow was," said Kirsty. "Now we have to find those goblins before they smash every present in the workshop. Let's go!"

Story Three
The Golden Present

Chapter Sixteen

Jimmy Barnes

The Cook's a Freak?

Chapter Eleven
Grumpy Elves

Rachel and Kirsty flew through the toy workshop and the wrapping room, but there was no sign of the goblins.

"We've peeped into every nook and cranny," said Rachel, fluttering down beside the chief elf. "It looks like they have gone."

"I hope you're right," said the chief elf. "We have lots of wrapping to finish."

The wrapping room was loud and busy, filled with the chatter of elves as they worked, and the crackle of paper and tape. Rachel and Kirsty hovered near a workbench that was covered with colourful ribbons.

"The presents look so exciting," said Kirsty.

"They're a waste of time and effort," the chief elf snapped. "I expect they won't even get played with. Children are ungrateful."

Rachel and Kirsty exchanged a shocked glance.

"I know you're wrong about that," said Rachel in a gentle voice. "Children get very excited about the presents they get from Father Christmas."

"I don't know why we bother," grumbled the chief elf.

She stomped away, knocking a ball of sparkly gold ribbon off the workbench. It rolled across the floor, glowing brightly as it unravelled.

"Rachel, look!" cried Kirsty.

Camilla sprang out from the tangled gold, holding the end of the ribbon. The three fairies hugged.

"I'm sorry," said Kirsty at once. "We haven't found the goblins or seen the golden present."

"Let's keep looking," said Camilla. "This is a very busy week for the Christmas Fairies. We're getting everything ready for the Fairyland Christmas Day party, and I need all my magical objects to be able to do my job. There will be music, dancing, wonderful food and a gift for every guest – even Jack Frost and the goblins. But if I don't find the golden present, Christmas generosity will vanish."

"We think the goblins must have gone," said Rachel.

"They can't have done," said Camilla. "The only way for them to leave the workshop is for Jack Frost to come and get them, and I've just seen him in Fairyland."

"Did he have the golden present?" asked Rachel.

"I didn't see it," Camilla replied. "But until I get it back, humans and fairies will feel mean and stingy."

"Elves too," said Rachel. "Just now, the chief elf was really grumpy about giving presents to children at Christmas."

"I've had an idea," Camilla said. "If the goblins aren't in the workshop or the wrapping room, maybe they've gone outside."

"But it's freezing out there on the mountain," said Kirsty.

"Don't be so sure," said Camilla.

She led Rachel and Kirsty past the elves, who were busy wrapping presents and muttering.

"What's the point of giving these nice presents to children?"

"I'm going to keep this one."

"We shouldn't have bothered."

"They all sound so grumpy," said Rachel.

Camilla listened carefully for a moment, and her implant seemed to sparkle even more brightly. Then she tapped her wand against one of the bricks in the wall of the room. The brick

shimmered, and then the whole wall started to swirl.

"It's unfolding," said Kirsty in amazement.

A hole appeared, and the fairies felt a blast of freezing air. They flew through, and the hole closed up behind them. Rachel and Kirsty gasped. Stretching out ahead, as far as the eye could see, was a vast, icy maze.

Chapter Twelve
Reindeer Rescue

"The Christmas Fairies built this special magic maze to help the elves to protect their secret workshop," Camilla explained. "Any mountain explorers who come close to the workshop will wander in here. They will be kept safe and warm until we can magic them back to the other side of the mountain."

"I love magic," said Rachel, for
the millionth time. "Has anyone ever
wandered in here by accident?"

"Only once," said Camilla. "We made
sure that they thought it was a dream.
The magic is warmest when we're inside.
Come on."

As they went in, Kirsty rested her hand
on the ice wall of the maze.

"It's warm, but it's not melting," she
said.

A giggle echoed ahead of them.

"They're in here," Kirsty exclaimed.

The fairies flew faster, turning corner
after corner. They heard more giggles
and squawks, but there was no sign of the
goblins. Then they turned another corner
and stopped.

"What's that?" asked Rachel.

There was a small, blue ball lying on the ground. Camilla reached out to pick it up.

"That's funny," said Kirsty. "It's exactly the same colour as Jack Frost's cloak."

Rachel gasped.

"What if it's a trick?" she said.
"Camilla, stop!"

It was too late. Camilla froze the second her fingers touched the blue ball. Before Rachel and Kirsty could reach her, Jack Frost stepped out from around the corner.

"Boo!" he said, and cackled with laughter.

"What have you done?" asked Kirsty. "Set Camilla free!"

Four goblins scampered up to Camilla and stood around her. Jack Frost glared at Rachel and Kirsty.

122

"I'm not letting fairies tell me what to do," he sneered. "She's coming with me to tell me how the golden present works."

There was a flash of blue lightning and a crash of thunder, and then Jack Frost, the goblins and Camilla vanished into thin air.

"They must have gone to Fairyland," said Rachel, fumbling for her locket. "Oh no!"

There were only a few specks of fairy dust left in the locket. Kirsty's was the same.

"Of course," said Kirsty. "We used most of it earlier, to turn ourselves into fairies."

"How are we going to reach Fairyland without fairy dust?" asked Rachel. "Camilla's gone."

"And the elves are too busy wrapping presents to check the maze," said Rachel. "We're stuck here."

A stamping sound came from above their heads. They looked up and gasped in astonishment. A huge reindeer was standing on top of the ice wall.

"Hello, reindeer," said Rachel.

The reindeer snorted and jumped gracefully down beside her.

"This is no ordinary reindeer," said Kirsty. "Its antlers are glowing."

The reindeer shook its head, and Rachel and Kirsty heard a jingling sound. Tiny golden bells were tied to its antlers with red ribbons.

"It's a Christmas reindeer," Rachel whispered. "And this is Christmas magic."

The reindeer knelt down on its front knees.

"I think it wants to give us a ride," said Kirsty, tingling with excitement.

They fluttered on to the reindeer's back and held on tight. With a mighty leap, the beautiful animal whooshed up into the sky.

Surrounded by glowing magic and the sound of jingling bells, Rachel and Kirsty zoomed across the sky, the wind blowing back their hair. Amazing colours streaked around them as the reindeer galloped faster and faster.

"Dear reindeer," shouted Rachel over the roar of the wind, "we need to go to Jack Frost's Castle."

Instantly, like the drop on a rollercoaster ride, they plunged downwards.

Chapter Thirteen
Frozen Fairy

Seconds later, the reindeer landed on a mound of fresh snow in Jack Frost's garden. There were frozen trees and snowflake-shaped bushes frosted with ice. The grim walls of Jack Frost's castle loomed over them. Rachel and Kirsty fluttered off the reindeer's back.

"Thank you for helping us," said Kirsty.

The reindeer lowered its head as if it were saying "You're welcome". Then it sprang into the sky. In a moment, it had disappeared.

"Now we have to find Camilla," said Kirsty.

"Listen," said Rachel. "I can hear squawking."

They fluttered around a hedge. The first thing they saw was a queue of goblins. It snaked around the Ice Lord, who was sitting on a throne of crystal-clear ice. Each goblin had a roughly wrapped present. Jack Frost was unwrapping them one after the other.

"Rubbish," Jack Frost yelled, throwing the present over his shoulder. "Next!"

Rachel and Kirsty fluttered closer and

ducked down behind a spiky bush. Jack Frost opened another present.

"Useless," he snarled, throwing it at the goblins.

"There's something under his throne," said Rachel.

They could just see a present wrapped in glowing golden paper, with curling ribbons and a big, sparkly bow.

"That must be the golden present," Kirsty said. "He's using its magic to make the goblins be generous to him."

Just then, the line of goblins broke up, squabbling and shoving each other.

"Look," Rachel exclaimed. "It's Camilla."

The line of goblins had been hiding her from view. She was still frozen.

"What's the matter with you all?" Jack Frost yelled at the goblins. "These gifts are stupid! A broken pencil? A pebble? I want proper presents!"

"We want to give you everything," one goblin called out. "We'll wrap everything up and give it you."

"Even if it doesn't belong to us," piped up another goblin.

"The goblins are being generous, but they don't have the glowing list or the glittering bow," Rachel whispered.

"Without Camilla's other magical objects, they don't know how to choose the perfect present or how to do beautiful wrapping."

"They're just feeling very generous," said Kirsty.

"We have to rescue Camilla and stop this," said Rachel. "Come on."

Together, the fairies flew out from their hiding place and landed in front of Jack Frost. He slowly rose up from his icy throne.

"What do you want?" he demanded. "Buzz off!"

"We want you to let Camilla go," said Rachel.

"No," Jack Frost retorted. "Why should I?"

Kirsty had a brainwave.

"Because you won't be able to go to the Fairyland Christmas party," she said.

Jack Frost's eyes almost popped out of his head.

"What Christmas party?" he growled.

"There's a party on Christmas Day," said Rachel. "But they won't have it if one of the Christmas Fairies is missing."

"That's right," said Kirsty. "There won't be any cakes or refreshments."

"Or music or dancing," Rachel added.

The goblins had started listening when

cakes were mentioned.

"No cakes?" squawked one of them.

Another goblin's bottom lip started to wobble.

"And no presents," Kirsty went on. "Not while the Christmas Present Fairy is missing. Everyone will be too stingy to want to give presents."

"I want to go to that party!" Jack Frost
yelled.

"The only way you can make the
party happen is by setting Camilla free,"
said Rachel.

Jack Frost folded his arms and scowled
at her. The girls held their breath. What
was he going to say?

Chapter Fourteen
Tower of Troublemakers

"No," said Jack Frost.

Rachel and Kirsty exchanged a look of alarm.

"What are we going to do?" asked Rachel. "We have no magic of our own, and no fairy dust."

Suddenly, Kirsty had an idea.

"We do have fairy dust," she said in a low voice. "There are a few specks left in our lockets. It's not much, but maybe it's enough magic to thaw Camilla."

"Great idea," said Rachel. "But how are we going to get close enough to sprinkle the fairy dust on to her?"

They flew towards Camilla.

"What are they doing?" Jack Frost shouted at the goblins. "Stop them!"

One goblin jumped on to another's shoulders and blocked their way. The fairies flew back.

"Ha!" Jack Frost snorted.

"I've got an idea," said Kirsty. "Let's get all the goblins to climb up to reach us. As soon as they're all on top of each other, we can swoop down to Camilla."

Rachel and Kirsty kept making little

darts towards
Camilla, higher
and higher. The
goblins clambered
on top of each
other's shoulders,
waving their
arms like wobbly
acrobats. They
swiped at the
fairies, but Rachel
and Kirsty stayed
just out of reach.

"It's working,"
Rachel whispered.

Soon the tower
of goblins was as
high as the ice-
covered trees. It

swayed wildly left and right. There was just one goblin left, and he began to climb.

"Now!" said Kirsty.

They dived towards Camilla and opened their lockets over her head. her hair and her implant. Had it worked?

Yes! Camilla took a deep breath and blinked.

"Thank goodness," she said. "Hey, how did we get to Jack Frost's Castle?"

"No!" Jack Frost bellowed.

The tower of goblins leaned sideways and then scattered across the grass, squawking and shouting. Rachel pulled Camilla and Kirsty behind a snow-covered bush.

"The golden present is under his throne," Kirsty told Camilla.

The throne was opposite them, but Jack Frost was sitting in it. There was no way to reach it without being seen.

"I have an idea how we can get it back," said Rachel. "Camilla, could you use your magic to melt the throne? It's on a bit of a slope. If we're lucky, the water might wash the golden present straight towards us."

Camilla waved her wand, and a warm breeze ruffled their hair. Instantly, the fairies stopped shivering. *DRIP! DRIP!* The snow on the trees, the frost on the grass and the icy throne all began to melt.

"Hey, why am I all wet?" Jack Frost exclaimed.

With a sudden splash, the throne collapsed on to the golden present. The stream of water flowed down the slope, carrying Camilla's magical object straight towards the fairies.

"Stop that water!" Jack Frost howled.

His goblins scrabbled across the wet grass, churning it into mud, but they were too slow. The golden present bobbed past

the bush, and Camilla scooped it up with a cry of joy. Jack Frost and the goblins sploshed towards them.

"I think it's time for us to go," said Rachel.

Before Camilla could raise her wand, a whoosh of sparkling fairy dust swept the fairies off their feet. Spinning rapidly, they were lifted into the sky and whisked away. Seconds later, they felt the ground beneath their feet again.

"Oh my goodness, I'm so dizzy," said Kirsty, giggling. "How did you do that, Camilla?"

"It wasn't Camilla," said a calm, steady voice. "It was me."

Chapter Fifteen
Friends For Ever

They were standing in the Fairyland Palace ballroom, and Queen Titania was smiling at them.

"Welcome back, Rachel and Kirsty," she said. "And well done – without you, Camilla would still be a prisoner."

Rachel and Kirsty curtseyed, and then

Queen Titania tapped their lockets with her wand.

"They are filled with fairy dust again," she said. "Thank you for everything you have done to help Camilla and save our Christmas party."

"It was our pleasure," said Rachel.

The queen smiled and then glided out of the room. Rachel and Kirsty looked around. The ballroom was decorated with garlands of green ivy, twisted together with holly leaves and berries. Tiny Christmas candles and silver stars hung in the air above them, lighting the room with flickering sparkles. At the far end of the room was the tree that Camilla had shown them, glimmering with decorations and surrounded by presents.

Camilla fluttered over to the tree and hung the golden present from one of its branches.

"Perfect," she said.

Rachel and Kirsty flew over to her and they shared a happy hug. Then Kirsty took a deep breath.

"Camilla, it's been wonderful to spend time with you," she said. "But now that your magical objects are safe, will you magic us back to Rachel's bedroom? There's something I'm longing to do."

"Of course," said Camilla. "Thank you both from the bottom of my heart. And Merry Christmas!"

She pointed her wand at one of the little silver stars, and it floated down to the floor. Then it started to grow larger and larger.

"It's as big as a door," said Kirsty.

"It is a door," said Camilla.

She ushered them towards the star with a wave of her hand. Rachel and Kirsty stepped through side by side, and a bright silver flash made them squeeze their eyes shut. Then the light faded.

"We're back in my bedroom in
Tippington," Rachel exclaimed, blinking.
They whirled around to look behind
them, but the star had disappeared.

"What an incredible adventure," said
Rachel, falling on to her bed with her
arms stretched out. "We rode a reindeer!"

"I've got one more surprise for you,"

said Kirsty.

She reached into her bag and pulled out the gift that she had made for her best friend.

"Even though it's not Christmas Day yet, I can't wait any longer to give this to you," she said. "Merry Christmas, Rachel. Thank you for being the best friend a girl could wish for."

Beaming with smiles, Rachel untied the ribbon and undid the wrapping paper. Kirsty felt as if she wanted to squeal. This was even more exciting than getting a present.

When Rachel saw the rainbow-coloured friendship bracelet that Kirsty had made, she gave her an enormous hug.

"I love it," she said. "Will you help me

to tie it on?"

As soon as the bracelet was on, Rachel dived into the drawer of her bedside table and brought out a little present topped with a red bow.

"Merry Christmas," she said, smiling. "I think you'll like it."

Kirsty burst into laughter when she

opened her gift. It was a rainbow-coloured friendship bracelet!

"Thank you," she said. "Friends for ever! Let's never take them off."

They kneeled side by side as Rachel tied Kirsty's bracelet on. Then they heard Mr Walker's voice.

"Is that you, girls?" he called from downstairs. "I didn't hear you come in. Would you like to come and help with the wrapping? It's going well now, and there's a box of Christmas biscuits to keep you going."

The girls jumped to their feet.

"I know that Christmas isn't all about getting presents," said Kirsty. "But I never realised what a great feeling it is to give presents."

"I can't wait to see Mum and Dad

opening their presents on Christmas morning," said Rachel. "But first, let's go and open that biscuit box. Yum!"

The End

**Now it's time for Kirsty and
Rachel to help ...**

Padma the Pirate Fairy

Read on for a sneak peek ...

"Just taste the salt in the air," said Rachel
Walker, holding on to the ship's rail. "I
love being at sea."

She put her head back and the warm
breeze blew back her hair. Her best
friend, Kirsty Tate, leaned forward over
the railings, watching the ship's prow
plunge through the water.

"I never thought I'd be standing on a
real pirate ship," she said. "What's the
name of this front part of the deck?"

"The forecastle," Rachel reminded her.

"Oh, yes, I remember," Kirsty replied.
"And the high deck at the back of

the ship is called the poop deck, and everything in between is the quarterdeck, right? Hey, I think I'm getting the hang of being a pirate."

"You forgot the main deck and the gun deck," said Rachel. "And then there's the mizzenmast and the mainmast and the foremast . . . but I can't remember which one is which."

"I think that means we're still landlubbers," said Kirsty with a laugh.

The ship was called the *Golden Galleon*, and it belonged to her dad's friend Jake. He had invited the Tate family on a sailing trip to Briny-on-Sea, which held the biggest pirate festival of the year. Best of all, Kirsty had been allowed to bring her best friend along.

"What exactly is Jake's job?" Rachel asked. "He's not a real pirate, is he?"

"He does pirate birthday parties on the ship, and he performs a show at all the pirate festivals," said Kirsty. "Oh, I think I hear him coming."

Hearing heavy footsteps behind them, they turned around and saw Jake with Mr Tate.

Read Padma the Pirate Fairy to find out what adventures are in store for Kirsty and Rachel!

Calling all parents, carers and teachers!
The Rainbow Magic fairies are here to help
your child enter the magical world of reading.
Whatever reading stage they are at, there's
a Rainbow Magic book for everyone!
Here is Lydia the Reading Fairy's guide to
supporting your child's journey at all levels.

Starting Out

1 Our Rainbow Magic Beginner Readers are perfect for first-time readers who are just beginning to develop reading skills and confidence. Approved by teachers, they contain a full range of educational levelling, as well as lively full-colour illustrations.

Developing Readers

2 Rainbow Magic Early Readers contain longer stories and wider vocabulary for building stamina and growing confidence. These are adaptations of our most popular Rainbow Magic stories, specially developed for younger readers in conjunction with an Early Years reading consultant, with full-colour illustrations.

Going Solo

3 The Rainbow Magic chapter books - a mixture of series and one-off specials - contain accessible writing to encourage your child to venture into reading independently. These highly collectible and much-loved magical stories inspire a love of reading to last a lifetime.

www.rainbowmagicbooks.co.uk

"Rainbow Magic got my daughter reading chapter books. Great sparkly covers, cute fairies and traditional stories full of magic that she found impossible to put down" - Mother of Edie (6 years)

"Florence LOVES the Rainbow Magic books. She really enjoys reading now" - Mother of Florence (6 years)

Read along the Reading Rainbow!

Well done – you have completed the book!

This book was worth 2 stars.

See how far you have climbed on the Reading Rainbow opposite.
The more books you read, the more stars you can colour in
and the closer you will be to becoming a Royal Fairy!

Do you want to print your own Reading Rainbow?

1) Go to the Rainbow Magic website

2) Download and print out the poster

3) Colour in a star for every book you finish
and climb the Reading Rainbow

4) For every step up the rainbow,
you can download your very own certificate

There's all this and lots more at
rainbowmagicbooks.co.uk

You'll find activities, stories, a special newsletter
AND you can search for the fairy with your name!